For Mom and Dad,
who made me a reader.
—ME

To Boy, thanks for all the support, always!
Stay Golden, Pony.
—JRS

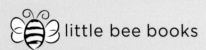 little bee books

New York, NY
Text copyright © 2022 by Melanie Ellsworth
Illustrations copyright © 2022 by James Rey Sanchez
All rights reserved, including the right of reproduction
in whole or in part in any form.
Manufactured in China RRD 0422
First Edition 10 9 8 7 6 5 4 3 2 1
Library of Congress Cataloging-in-Publication Data is available upon request.
ISBN 978-1-4998-1272-5
littlebeebooks.com

For information about special discounts on bulk purchases,
please contact Little Bee Books at sales@littlebeebooks.com.

BATTLE OF THE BOOKS

Written by
Melanie Ellsworth

Art by
James Rey Sanchez

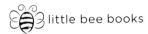 little bee books

On Josh's bookshelf, books flapped their pages,
wiggled their spines, and jostled for the best position.

"**Ahoy, me hearties! I'm on the top shelf
because I'm shipshape,**" said Pirate Book.
"**I wager Josh will be pickin' me for story time tonight!**"

"Slander!" cried Poem Book.
"Let me through! Roses are red. Violets are blue.
Josh will pick me. He will not pick you."

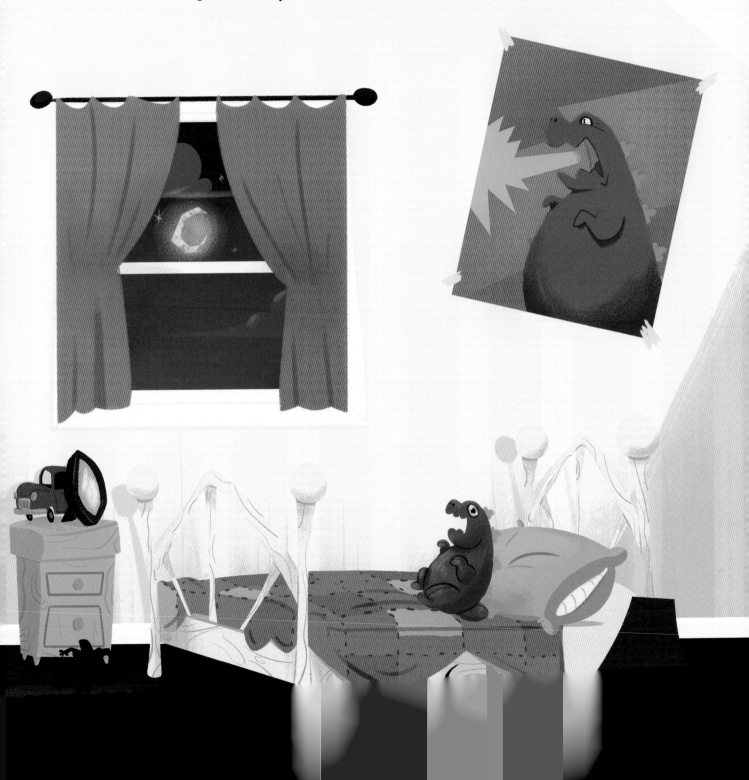

"**Aaarrgghhh,**" said Pirate Book.
"**Josh wants a rousin' tale with deadly swords
and treasure hoards!**"

"*Well, I may be on the middle shelf,*" said Joke Book,
sticking out his tongue, "*but at least I make Josh laugh!*"

"Josh doesn't want a laugh—he wants a liftoff!
A space-tastic adventure!" said Space Book.
"I blast him to the stars and beyond!"

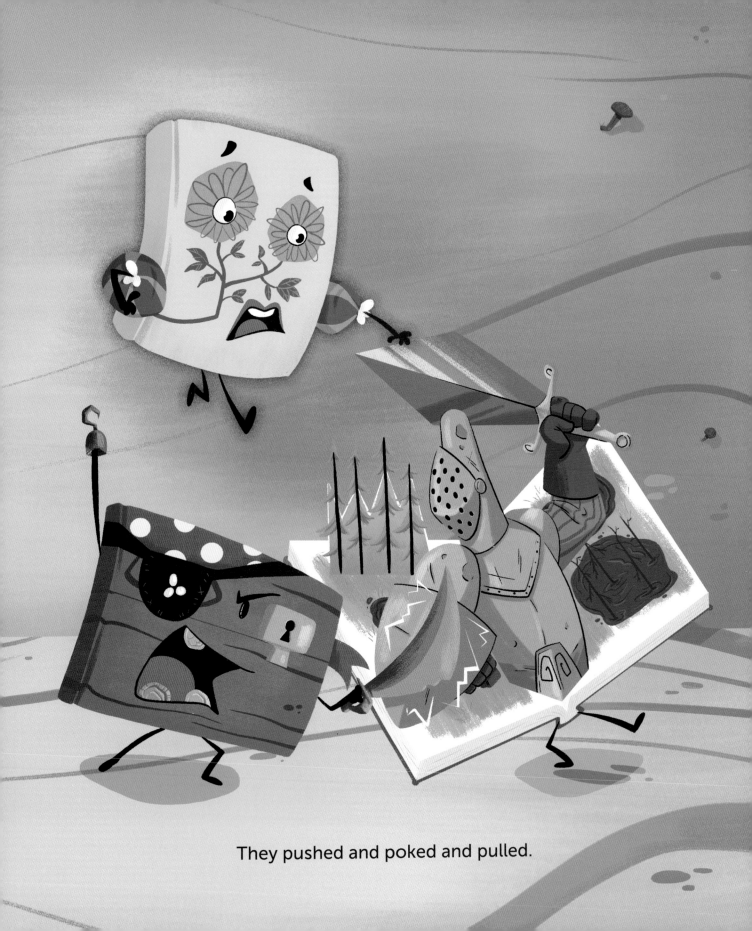

They pushed and poked and pulled.

Pop-Up Book sprang to the edge of the shelf.
"I'm fancy! I even got a design award."

"Aye, ye did," snorted Pirate Book.
"But ye got no story. Ye got no hook!"

"Josh picked me last night because I'm dino-mite,"
boasted Dinosaur Book.

"Ye just got lucky, matey!

"You're just a *saur loser*," Dinosaur Book roared.
"Walk the plank!"

Cheers erupted on the bookshelf.

"WHAM! BAM! One book down!" shouted Joke Book.

"Ye scallywags! That's mutiny!" cried Pirate Book.
"Just ye wait till I'm back on the shelf!!!"

Pirate Book flapped around on the floor.

"Shiver me timbers! It be dark down here.
Thar be sharks under the bed!"

Snuffle, sniff.

"Is that a sob I hear, Pirate dear?" asked Poem Book,
peering over the shelf.

"Ye scurvy dog! Pirates never cry," sobbed Pirate Book.
"I've just got a bit of salt in me eye."

Poem Book sighed. "Let's make amends, my friends,
and send some cheer to our brave buccaneer."

ZOOM! ZIP! Joke Book raced to the rescue.

"Here's a joke for you. What do you call a pirate
with two hands, two eyes, and two legs? . . . . A beginner!"

"Yo-ho-hiccup!"

"ROAR!!!"

bellowed Dinosaur Book.
"Did that scare the sharks away?"

"That helped a mite, matey."

"Let's rescue Pirate!" suggested Pop-Up Book.
"I'm sending down my spectacularly designed staircase!"

"You can do it, Pirate. 3—2—1—blast off!" called Space Book.

"I'll share an inspirational poem," said Poem Book.
"Heave, ho, and up you go! Heave, ho, and up you go!"

PLUNK! Pirate Book landed on the shelf.
The bookshelf once again erupted in cheers.

"Thanks, mateys. Ye be a fine crew."

"Roar! And, umm . . . *saur-y* for pushing you off the shelf,"
murmured Dinosaur Book.

"Forgotten!" growled Pirate Book.
"Avast, mateys! Footsteps in the hall!
Batten down the hatches!"

"Which one of us will Josh pick to read tonight? The end's in sight to our bookish plight! May the best story achieve glory!" cried Poem Book.

"Aye—that'd be me," said Pirate Book with a wink.
Poem Book elbowed Pirate Book.

"Don't bet your doubloons on it, Pirate!"

The bedroom door opened, and Josh and Grammie skipped in.

"Story time," sang out Grammie.
"Look what I brought for you, Josh—this book was
my favorite when I was your age!"

"DOOM! GLOOM! A Grammie pick.
It's curtains for us," said Joke Book.

"Aye, the top shelf's no good now.
We might as well be shark bait," sighed Pirate Book.
Their spines sagged.

"But Grammie, these are *my* favorite books. Can we read them, too?"

"All of them, Josh?" Grammie laughed. "Well . . . all right!"

The books huddled together and listened to story after story. Slowly, they drifted off, dreaming of tomorrow's tales and the next . . .

BATTLE OF THE BOOKS